This igloo book belongs to:

igloobooks

Published in 2021
First published in the UK by Igloo Books Ltd
An imprint of Igloo Books Ltd
Cottage Farm, NN6 0BJ, UK
Owned by Bonnier Books
Sveavägen 56, Stockholm, Sweden
www.igloobooks.com

0221 001
2 4 6 8 10 9 7 5 3 1
ISBN 978-1-80022-644-9

Written by Stephanie Moss
Illustrated by Jeff Crowther

Designed by Alex Alexandrou
Edited by Stephanie Moss

Printed and manufactured in China

WANTED
Shark

igloobooks

The day was here at last. Meg's big dream was coming true!
But when she saw the little fish, she wondered what to do.

The shop assistant chuckled. Then he smiled and shook his head. **"We've got a lovely goldfish here that you can have instead!"**

Meg was disappointed. This wasn't right at all. She just wanted a great **big** shark! This fish was super small.

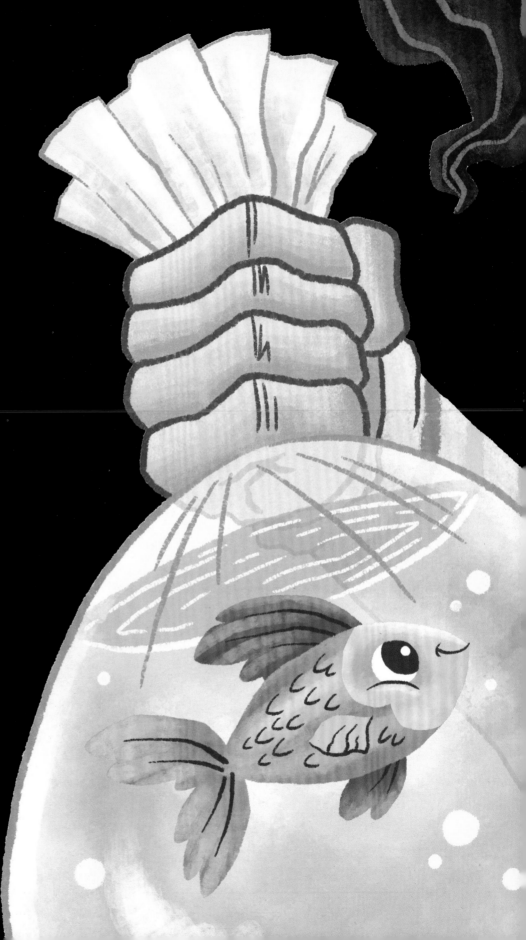

So, she put him in his little bowl and made a special wish.

"Please turn into a **MASSIVE** shark, and not a tiny fish."

When she woke up
in the morning, Meg was
in for a surprise.

Her goldfish had transformed.
A shark was there before her eyes!

"Hi, I'm Meg!" she told him, shaking his fin in her hand.

"I'd love to show you round, as long as you're here on dry land?"

Shark grinned a toothy smile, so Meg flashed him one right back.

Then they
both sat down to
breakfast for a sharky
morning snack.

Next, Shark had a bath,
and brushed his teeth
until they shone.
"We'll be home for tea!"
called Meg, and with that,
they were gone.

They tried on
silly outfits
and rode fun rides
at the park.

They even shared
an ice cream that
was just too big
for Shark!

He taught Meg how to dive in from the high board at the pool.

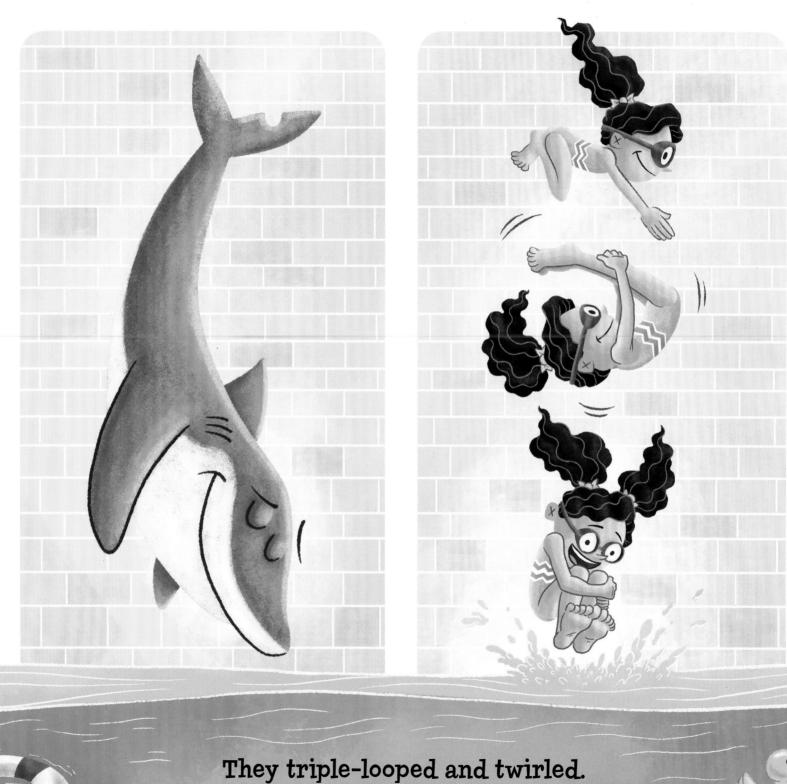

They triple-looped and twirled.
Then Meg called, **"That was super cool!"**

"Will you meet MY friends?" asked Shark,
and Meg said, "Yes, yippee!"
They ran along the pier and then they jumped into the sea.

They dived deeper
through the water till they
reached the sandy floor.
There were so many creatures
Meg had never seen before!

"**Welcome to Shark City!**" he said. "**Have a look around.**"
It was nothing like the boring world they'd left above the ground.

They sang shark-araoke. Then they played shark hide-and-seek.
And did you know that sharks go to the dentist twice a week?

"Tonight's our sunset party and we're having bubble stew!"

Shark said mermaids join in and that Meg should be there, too.

So, they swam back to the surface and went surfing in the sun.
Meg knew that sharks were awesome, but never this much fun.

Then, before she knew it, it was time to say goodbye.

"I'll miss you, Meg,"
her friend Shark said,
as he tried not to cry.

Meg got what she wanted,
and she'd loved their time together.
Although Shark couldn't stay,
he'd be Meg's best friend forever.